The Golden Books Treasury of
Christmas Joy

Favorite Stories, Poems,
Carols, and more

Compiled and Edited by **Skip Skwarek**

Illustrated by **Valerie Sokolova**

A Golden Book ~ New York

Golden Books Publishing Company, Inc. New York, New York 10106

With thanks to my Mom and Dad
for happy Christmases past and to come—S.S.

With love and thanks to my Mom and Dad,
Larisa and Stanislav Sokolov,
for all of their help, encouragement, and inspiration—V.S.

Acknowledgments

The compiler and publisher have made every effort to trace the ownership of all copyrighted
material and to secure permission from copyright holders. Any errors or omissions are inadvertent,
and the publisher will be pleased to make the necessary corrections in future printings.
Thanks to the following authors and publishers for their permission to use the material indicated:

"Apple Tree Christmas," copyright 1985 by Trinka Hakes Noble. Used by permission of
Dial Books for Young Readers, a division of Penguin Putnam, Inc.

"The Bearer of Gifts," text copyright 1998 by Kenneth Steven. Used by permission of
Dial Books for Young Readers, a division of Penguin Putnam, Inc.

"A Christmas Miracle," copyright 1996 by Robert D. San Souci. Used by permission of the author.

Library of Congress Cataloging-in-Publication Data
The Golden Books treasury of Christmas joy /
compiled by Skip Skwarek ; illustrated by Valerie Sokolova.
p. cm.
Summary: An illustrated collection of stories, poems, carols,
recipes, and crafts celebrating the spirit of Christmas.
ISBN 0-307-16855-7 (alk. paper)
1. Christmas—Literary collections. [1. Christmas—Literary collections.]
I. Skwarek, Skip. II. Sokolova, Valerie, ill.
PZ5.G5663 2001   808.8'0334—dc21   00-021406

The artwork was prepared with watercolor, gouache, colored pencil, and airbrush.

Contents

Part One

CHRISTMAS IS COMING!

Somehow not only for Christmas
But all the long year through,
The joy that you give to others
Is the joy that comes back to you.

And the more you spend in blessing
The poor and lonely and sad,
The more of your heart's possessing
Returns to make you glad.

—*from an untitled poem*
John Greenleaf Whittier

A Christmas Carol
Deck the Halls

*T*his jolly old carol, known and loved worldwide, originated in Wales. The tune was used by Mozart in the eighteenth century in a set of variations for the violin and piano.

Words traditional / Traditional Welsh melody

With spirit

1. Deck the halls with boughs of hol - ly,
2. See the blaz - ing Yule be - fore us,   } Fa, la, la, la, la, la, la, la, la.
3. Fast a - way the old year pass - es,

'Tis the sea - son to be jol - ly,
Strike the harp and join the cho - rus,   } Fa, la, la, la, la, la, la, la, la.
Hail the new, ye lads and lass - es,

Don we now our gay ap - par - el,
Fol - low me in mer - ry meas - ure,   } Fa, la, la, la, la, la, la, la, la.
Sing we joy - ous all to - geth - er,

Troll the an - cient Yule - tide ca - rol,
While I tell of Yule - tide treas - ure,   } Fa, la, la, la, la, la, la, la, la.
Heed-less of the wind and weath - er,

Christmas Around the World

by Skip Skwarek

Christ's birth has been celebrated in December since the fourth century. Some symbols of the holiday, such as the star of Bethlehem and the manger scene, are known and loved by all. But every country also has its own special symbols and traditions. In America, people wish each other "Merry Christmas," write to Santa Claus, and celebrate Christ's birth on Christmas Eve or Christmas Day. In other countries . . .

Happy Christmas!

English children write letters to Father Christmas. Instead of being mailed, letters are put into the fireplace and burned. The smoke finds its way to Father Christmas, who can "read" the children's wishes in the smoke.

¡Feliz Navidad!
(feh-*leeth* nah-vee-*dad*)

In Spain, on the feast of the Epiphany, children fill their shoes with hay for the camels of the three Wise Men and set them outside. The next morning, the hay has disappeared and children find their shoes filled with candy and gifts.

Joyeux Noël!
(zhoi-yew no-elle)

After midnight Mass on Christmas Eve, many French families celebrate Christ's birth with a grand feast called *le reveillon*, which reminds them to 'wake up' to the holiday's true meaning. For dessert, a cake, shaped and decorated to look like a Yule log, is often served.

Buon Natale!
(bwon na-tah-leh)

In Italian villages, the whole family helps to set up their *presepio*, or manger scene. Figures of the Holy Family, Wise Men, shepherds, and animals are placed in an elaborate handmade landscape with trees, hills, a river or lake, and even a starry sky.

Frohe Weihnachten!
(fro-e vy-nock-tin)

Some German children leave letters on their windowsills for the *Christkind*, an angel in a white robe and golden crown who brings gifts on Christmas Eve. To make them easier to spot, the letters are often decorated with sugar sprinkled on glue to make them sparkle.

Wesołych Świąt!
(veh-*so*-wih shfyont)

In honor of the star of Bethlehem, Christmas Eve dinners in Poland do not begin until the first star appears in the night sky. A bit of hay is placed beneath the tablecloth in memory of the Holy Child's birthplace, and an extra place is set for Him at the table.

Gelukkig Kerstfeest!
(hah-*loo*-kah *kerst*-face)

On December 5, Sinter Klass rides through the streets of the Netherlands on a snowy white horse. Children leave their wooden shoes or *sabots* outside, filled with hay for his horse. The next morning, if they've been good, they'll find gifts and sweets in their shoes.

Gledelig Jul!
(gly-*deh*-lig yool)

On Christmas Eve, Norwegian children remember to put out a bowl of special porridge for Nissa, a gnome who protects all the farm animals. It is said that Nissa enjoys playing tricks on children who forget to leave him his treat.

Hauskaa Joulua!
(*ha-oos*-kah *yo*-loo-wah)

*I*n Finland, the ground is covered by deep snow all winter long. Before sitting down to their own Christmas dinners, children strew nuts and seeds over the crusty snow and tie sheaves of grain to tall poles as a feast for the hungry birds.

¡Feliz Navidad!
(feh-*leece* nah-vee-*dad*)

*O*n the nine nights before Christmas, Mexican children march in candlelit parades called *las posadas*, reenacting Joseph and Mary's search for lodging. Then, each gets a chance to break open a *piñata*, a gaily decorated clay container filled with gifts and sweets.

Maligayang Pasko!
(mah-lay-*gah*-yen pass-*ko*)

*I*n the Philippine Islands, where the weather is always warm, decorations of fresh flowers are popular. Children make wreaths and chains of beautiful tropical flowers to wear as they walk from house to house singing Christmas songs.

Christmas ABC

by Florence Johnson

is for angels
from Heaven above.

is for bells,
ringing news of God's love.

is for candy canes,
striped red and white.

is for Dancer, on a
round-the-world flight.

15

is for evergreen,
topped with a star.

is for frankincense
brought from afar.

is for gifts,
a joy to give and receive.

is for holly
with its festive green leaves.

is for icicles,
agleam in the sun.

is for Jesus,
the Holiest One.

is for king,
three set off on a quest.

is for lantern,
to welcome each guest.

is for mistletoe,
inviting kisses sweet.

is for neighbors,
sharing holiday treats.

17

is for ornaments,
glistening gold overhead.

is for poinsettia,
starlike petals bright red.

is for quilt,
for your long winter's nap.

is for ribbon,
trimming presents you wrap.

is for Santa Claus,
stockings, and sleigh.

is for toys,
brand new on Christmas Day.

is for underwear,
red flannel and long.

is for voices,
raised in holiday song.

19

W is for wreath,
adorned with candles and holly.

X is for kisses
to that old elf so jolly.

Y is for Yule log,
giving warmth and good cheer.

Z is for *ZOOM!*
Santa's off till next year.

A Christmas Craft
Blooming Gifts

*A*n amaryllis in full bloom makes an eye-catching Christmas decoration or an impressive (and inexpensive) gift. Planting and tending is simple enough for children as young as six, and all ages will watch with delight as the budded stem and leaves shoot up from the bulb almost as quickly as Jack's beanstalk. Blooming begins six to eight weeks after planting. Buy good quality firm bulbs (the bigger the better) from a local garden center. There are many lovely varieties to choose from. "Peppermint Stick," with crimson swirls on white petals, is perfect for Christmas.

What you'll need for each bulb:

* a pot 3-4" larger in diameter than the bulb, and a drainage saucer
* pebbles or broken crockery for the bottom of the pot
* houseplant potting soil mix containing peat moss

Directions:

1) Cover pot's drainage hole with pebbles or broken crockery and fill at least halfway with soil.

2) Place bulb, root end down, on soil in pot. Add soil around bulb, leaving top third of bulb exposed. Top of soil should be about 1" from pot rim for ease of watering. Gently tamp down soil. Water well, but avoid pouring water directly on top of bulb.

3) Place pot in a warm, bright spot—near a south or west window is best. Water sparingly until first shoot appears, then keep evenly moist but not soggy. Give pot a quarter turn every few days to encourage stem and leaves to grow upright.

4) Once buds begin to open, pot can be moved to any location. A cooler spot with less direct light prolongs blooming. Remove flowers as they fade.

Apple Tree Christmas

by Trinka Hakes Noble

The Ansterburgs lived in the end of an old barn. Underneath, Mrs. Wooly and her lambs softly moved about, Old Dan bumped in his stall, and Sweet Clover mooed at milking time. On the first floor, Mama cooked on a big black stove and Papa worked in his woodshop, and above, Katrina and Josie slept in the hayloft. Someday Papa would build them a real house. But for now, living in the barn with the soft animal sounds and sweet smell of hay was just right.

Near the barn was an old apple tree. It was overgrown with wild grape vines, but Papa never cut away the vines because they made a natural ladder to the highest apples. "Besides," he always joked, "I could never separate such close friends."

"Girls, we'll be picking apples soon," said Mama one day.

"Maybe sooner than you think," said Papa. "I heard they got a foot of snow up north."

"Oh, dear," fretted Mama, "winter so soon."

"We'd better get the apples in tomorrow," said Papa.

"And I'll make a big batch of apple butter," said Mama. "You girls should stay home from school to help sort apples."

"Hurray!" shouted Katrina and Josie.

The next morning the ground was white, but even in the snow, sorting apples was fun. Some went into a pile for cider and applesauce, some went into baskets for pies, small ones were for their lunch pails, and the bruised ones were for Old Dan. But finding the apples to decorate their Christmas tree was what Katrina and Josie liked the best. All day long they picked and sorted until the most beautiful apples of all stood on the stone wall. Then Mama chose the biggest one.

"This will make a nice clove apple for our Christmas dinner table," she said. They wrapped the rest of the apples in cloth, and Papa put them in the bottom of the barn to keep until Christmas.

Now that all the apples were picked, Katrina and Josie could climb the tree as much as they wanted. The snowy weather didn't stop them. Every day after school they would play in its branches.

On one side, Papa had pulled a thick vine down low enough to make a swing for Josie.

The other side of the tree belonged to Katrina. One limb made a perfect drawing board. She called it her studio. There she would dream and draw until the cold winter sun glowed low behind the trees.

"Time for chores," called Mama as she lit the lantern.

Katrina and Josie ran inside the barn and climbed down the ladder to the animals' stalls. First they shelled corn for the hens, then they fed and watered Old Dan. They saved Mrs. Wooly and her family until last so they could stick their cold fingers deep into her wool coat.

"How warm you are, Mrs. Wooly," said Katrina.

"Just as warm as the scarf and socks we're knitting for Papa's Christmas presents, right, Katrina?" asked Josie.

"Shhh! He might hear you," scolded Katrina.

But Papa didn't hear them. He was busy putting Mrs. Wooly and her family in with Old Dan and Sweet Clover.

"Papa, what are you doing?" asked Katrina.

"We'll put the stock together tonight so they can keep warm. You climb up and stuff straw in those holes. It must have dropped twenty degrees in the last hour," said Papa.

"Do you think we'll have a blizzard?" asked Katrina.

"Wouldn't be a bit surprised. Probably be forty below by morning."

Katrina could feel the north wind blowing through the holes in the barn. Papa spread a thick layer of straw around the animals. Then he watered them again because by morning their trough would be frozen solid.

It was cold upstairs, too, but Mama had moved the table close to the stove, and a hot supper of apple fritters and maple syrup soon warmed them up.

That night the blizzard hit with full force. The old barn shook and its beams creaked as if they were in pain. In the loft Katrina woke with a start. She could hear Papa and Mama talking softly below. "Probably be gone by morning," Papa said. So she snuggled closer to Josie and went back to sleep.

But the blizzard got worse and lasted for three days and nights. On the third night something strange woke Katrina. The wind was howling and the beams were screaming, but there was a different sound, one more frightening—like a million sharp knives slashing the roof, cutting the barn, trying to get in.

Katrina was so frightened that she began to scream, but Mama and Papa were already there wrapping them up in quilts.

"Papa, what's happening?" asked Katrina, shaking with fright.

"Ice storm. We're moving you girls downstairs in case the roof caves in under the weight."

Mama put Katrina and Josie on a feather bed under the table. "Now try to sleep," she said.

But Katrina couldn't fall asleep. The ice storm tore at the barn, and throughout the night, Katrina was startled by the loud splintering sounds of big limbs snapping like twigs.

When Mama opened the stove door to add more wood, the firelight made an eerie orange glow. Her shadow looked big and strange. Katrina knew Mama would keep the fire going—no matter what.

The next morning there was calm. The storm had passed. Katrina was glad until she saw Papa's long face when he came inside.

"Ice storm took the old apple tree," he said.

"But surely the vines would hold it together," said Mama.

"No, it split right down through the middle. I'll chop it up for firewood," said Papa.

Katrina ran to the window. Through her tears she saw nothing but a heap of snow and ice and dead branches.

Every morning Papa brought in another pile of firewood and vines from the apple tree. Mama said they should keep busy knitting Papa's Christmas presents. Josie finished Papa's scarf and made one for Mama, too. Katrina worked on Mama's pincushion, but she just couldn't concentrate on knitting Papa's socks while he sawed and hacked away at the apple tree. She had ripped out the heel and started over so many times, she had all but ruined the yarn from Mrs. Wooly.

"Well, I'll miss the old apple tree," said Mama, "but it will keep us warm this long winter."

"Yes, I'm thankful for the firewood," said Papa.

How could he be thankful, thought Katrina. *Didn't he know that he was chopping up her studio? Didn't he know he was ruining her drawing board? Didn't he know she couldn't draw unless she was in the apple tree?*

On the day before Christmas, Mama made her clove apple and began baking pies. Papa brought in a fresh pine tree and they decorated it with the beautiful apples. But to Katrina it just didn't feel like Christmas. Even when she went to bed that night, Papa was still sawing away at the apple tree.

On Christmas morning the girls' stockings were stuffed with oranges, wild hickory nuts, black walnuts, and peppermint sticks. Josie gave Papa and Mama their scarves, and Katrina gave Mama the pincushion. But it still didn't feel like Christmas to Katrina.

Then Papa said, "Now my little ones, turn around and close your eyes. No peeking."

First Katrina heard Papa whisper to Mama to help him. Next she heard him hammering something to the beam, then he dragged something across the floor.

"All right, you can look now," said Mama.

They whirled around.

There, hanging from the beam, was Josie's swing, the very same vine swing from the apple tree. Sitting on the swing was a little rag doll that Mama had made.

Near the swing was a drawing board made from the very same limb that had been Katrina's studio. On the drawing board were real charcoal paper and three sticks of willow charcoal.

Katrina softly touched the drawing board. She wanted to say, *How wise and wonderful you are, Papa,* and *Thank you, Papa,* and *I'll always love you, Papa.* But all she could say was, "Oh, Papa."

Papa didn't say anything. He just handed her the three sticks of charcoal.

Josie began to swing with her doll and Katrina started to draw. Now she could see how beautiful Mama's clove apple looked on the white tablecloth, and how shiny red the apples were on the Christmas tree. Now she could smell the fresh winter pine tree and the warm apple pies. Now it felt like Christmas.

Katrina gave her first drawing to Papa. It was a picture of the day when Papa picked the apples and Mama made apple butter and Katrina and Josie sorted the apples.

In the corner of the picture Papa wrote:

This picture was drawn by
Katrina Ansterburg on Christmas Day 1881.

Then he hung it in his woodshop and there it stayed for many long years.

Don't Look!

Don't look in the closets,
Or under the beds,
Or in any mysterious nook
Where things may be hidden—
It's simply forbidden
When Christmas is coming—
Don't look!

Don't take up a package
That comes in the mail,
And give it a squeeze or a shake
To guess what's inside it
Before they can hide it—
That's really a Christmas
Mistake.

Don't listen at bedtime
To hear what they're saying,
Or peep in when doors are ajar.
Hold your ears, shut your eyes,
For a Christmas surprise
Is better on Christmas,
By far!

—*Kathryn Jackson*

A Christmas Craft
Pop-Up Christmas Cards

𝒫rinted Christmas cards first appeared in England over 100 years ago. Today, people all over the world send these holiday greetings. Making your own is easy, inexpensive, and fun. The Santa and Christmas tree shown on these pages are just the right size for your cards. Trace them if you wish, or use your imagination and come up with your own ideas!

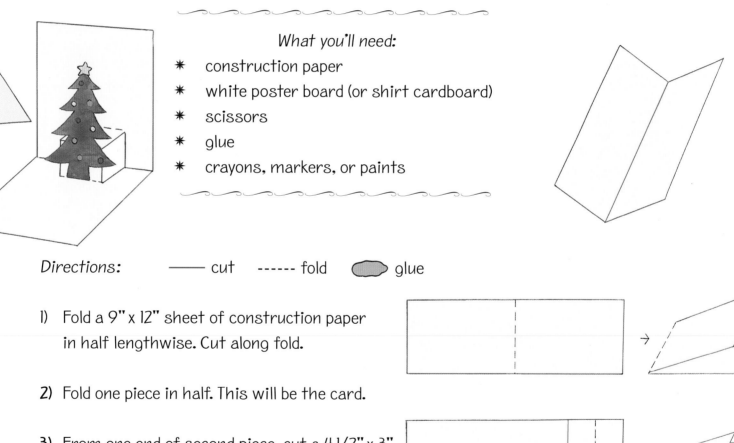

What you'll need:

* construction paper
* white poster board (or shirt cardboard)
* scissors
* glue
* crayons, markers, or paints

Directions: —— cut ------ fold ⬭ glue

1) Fold a 9" x 12" sheet of construction paper in half lengthwise. Cut along fold.

2) Fold one piece in half. This will be the card.

3) From one end of second piece, cut a 4 1/2" x 3" section, fold in half, and set aside.

4) In middle of card's folded edge, make 2 cuts, about 1" long and 1" apart.

5) Fold cut section up like a tab and crease firmly. Then fold tab back down.

6) Open card and push cut section from behind so it pops up inside. It will look like a step.

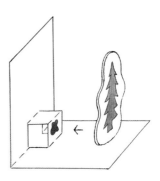
pop-up can be this tall

7) On poster board or shirt cardboard, draw what you want to pop up in your card. Don't make it taller than the space shown or it will stick out when card is closed. Color and cut out.

8) Glue it to front of pop-up step in card. Close card and press down firmly.

9) Put glue on reserved piece of folded construction paper as shown.

10) Slide reserved piece over folded edge of closed card to hide step hole. Press down firmly.

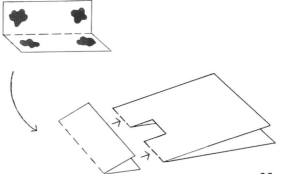

11) Draw and color a picture on front of card, and don't forget to write your Christmas greeting inside.

Cranberry Cashew Caramel Corn

This is so scrumptious, you may need several batches!

Dried cranberries add festive color to this quick-to-make treat. Pack it in decorative tins for gift-giving or form into old-fashioned popcorn balls to hang on the Christmas tree.

Ingredients:

1/2 cup unpopped popcorn	2 tablespoons butter or margarine
oil for popping (optional)	1 pound light brown sugar
1 1/2 cups dried cranberries	2/3 cup water
1 1/2 cups salted cashew pieces	1 teaspoon cinnamon

Directions:

1) Pop corn using your favorite method.
2) Combine popped corn, cranberries, and nuts in a 6-quart mixing bowl.
3) In a 1-quart heavy-bottomed saucepan, melt butter over low heat. Add sugar, water, and cinnamon, and stir until sugar is dissolved. Brush down sugar crystals from sides of pan with a pastry brush dipped in warm water. Increase heat to medium, and boil mixture without stirring until it reaches the soft-crack stage (270° on a candy thermometer).
4) Remove syrup from heat and drizzle over popcorn mixture. (Be careful—syrup is very hot!) Stir quickly with a wooden spoon until mixture is well coated.
5) Spread on cookie sheets lined with wax paper to cool completely. Store in airtight containers.

For Popcorn Balls

When mixture is just cool enough to handle, rub a little butter on hands and quickly form handfuls of mixture into balls. When completely cool, wrap each in tinted or clear plastic wrap and secure with ribbon tied into a bow.

Yield: about 4 quarts or 24 handful-size balls

Part Two

O CHRISTMAS TREE!

Now gay trees rise
Before young eyes
Abloom with tempting cheer;
Blithe voices sing,
And blithe bells ring,
For Christmas-tide is here.

Oh, happy chime,
Oh, blessed time,
That draws us all so near!
"Welcome, dear day,"
All creatures say,
For Christmas-tide is here.

—*from* A Christmas Dream, and How It Came True
Louisa May Alcott

The Lights on the Christmas Tree

by Florence Page Jaques

*L*ong, long ago when Santa Claus trimmed the very first Christmas tree, there were no strings of colored lights. In fact, all the decorations Santa used were white. He has always lived at the North Pole, you know, where the ground is covered with ice and snow all year long. So Santa decorated the first Christmas tree with things he found right outside his workshop door. He wrapped it with garlands of glistening icicles, tied frosty snowballs to the ends of its branches, and sprinkled it with handfuls of newly fallen snowflakes. When he'd finished, Santa stepped back to admire his work. "Hmmm," he said to himself. "It's pretty, but it could use a little color . . . a bit of red and green and blue and yellow—"

"What about a rainbow?" suggested Littlest White Bear, who had stopped to watch on his way home from ice-fishing school.

"That's just what it needs," agreed Santa. "I'll ask Biggest White Bear to get one for me."

"Oh, let me get it!" cried Littlest White Bear, who was always being told he was too little to do things. "Please, Santa. It was my idea!"

"Well, all right then," Santa said kindly. "But you must carry it *very* carefully. Rainbows are easy to break, you know."

"I will be *very, very* careful," promised Littlest White Bear. Then he ran as quickly as his short little legs would carry him all the way to the edge of the icy sea, where the spray from the waves splashed up and turned into rainbows. Littlest White Bear chose the rainbow with the brightest shimmering colors. He lifted it very, very carefully and hung it around his neck. Then he crept off the slick ice floe very, very carefully, making sure not to bump into any icebergs. He made his way very, very carefully through the snowy fields, staying safely away from slippery drifts. And at last he saw the workshop and Santa waving from the front steps.

"I got it!" shouted Littlest White Bear, waving his front paws at Santa. "Here is the rainbow!"

But just then both of his back paws skidded on the tiniest bit of ice, and Littlest White Bear fell—*kerplunk!*—right on his backside. At the same time, the rainbow slipped from around his neck and shattered into a thousand pieces. "Oh! Oh! Oh!" cried Littlest White Bear.

"Oh, oh, oh, my!" said Santa, rushing to the fallen bear. "You aren't hurt, are you?"

"No, but the rainbow is," sobbed Littlest White Bear, "and I tried so hard to be careful."

Santa picked up a piece of the broken rainbow. It glowed in the sunlight. "Dry your tears," he said to Littlest White Bear. "These pieces are just the right size!"

"For what?" asked Littlest White Bear, wiping his eyes.

"Help me put them on the tree," replied Santa, placing rainbow pieces here and there on the higher branches. Littlest White Bear put pieces here, there, and everywhere on the lower branches. Before long the tree glowed with spots of rainbow color from top to bottom.

"It's so beautiful!" murmured Littlest White Bear.

"It was your idea," chuckled Santa.

"Yes!" Littlest White Bear agreed proudly. "It was my idea to fall down, too!"

And that is how we came to have beautiful rainbow-colored lights on the Christmas tree.

A Christmas Carol
O Christmas Tree

The words to this German carol originated in 1824. The tune is said to be one of the oldest-known melodies. The custom of decorating fir trees at Christmas began in Germany during the time of Martin Luther.

Traditional German tune / Arranged by Norman Lloyd

Sweetly

1. O Christ - mas Tree, O Christ - mas Tree, Your branch - es green de - light us. O
2. O Christ - mas Tree, O Christ - mas Tree, You give us so much plea - sure! O

Christ - mas Tree, O Christ - mas Tree, Your branch - es green de - light us. They're
Christ - mas Tree, O Christ - mas Tree, You give us so much plea - sure! How

green when sum - mer days are bright; They're green when win - ter snow is white. O
oft at Christ - mas - tide the sight, O green fir tree, gives us de - light! O

Christ - mas Tree, O Christ - mas Tree, Your branch - es green de - light us.
Christ - mas Tree, O Christ - mas Tree, You give us so much plea - sure!

41

Orange Ginger Rolled Cookies

Set some aside to hang on the tree as charming, edible ornaments.

*T*hese are crisp, fragrant with spices, and fun to make. Cut them in Christmas shapes with cookie cutters, or in simple shapes with a knife. Decorate before baking with raisins, currants, nuts, chocolate chips, or colored sugar; or ice with your favorite cookie icing after baking. Younger children will enjoy helping with the cutting out and decorating. Older ones can handle these from start to finish.

Ingredients:

1 cup (2 sticks) unsalted butter, softened
1 1/2 cups granulated sugar
3 tablespoons unsulphured molasses
1 large egg
2 tablespoons milk
1 teaspoon pure orange extract
1 tablespoon grated orange rind

3 1/2 cups unbleached flour
2 teaspoons baking soda
1/2 teaspoon salt
2 teaspoons ground ginger
2 teaspoons cinnamon
1/2 teaspoon ground cloves
1/2 teaspoon ground cardamom

Directions:

1) In a large bowl, beat butter, sugar, and molasses until light and smooth. Add egg, milk, orange extract, and grated orange rind. Blend well.

2) In a separate bowl, combine flour, baking soda, salt, and spices. Gradually beat flour mixture into butter mixture just until combined.

3) Remove dough from bowl with floured hands and knead briefly. Divide into halves, wrap each tightly in plastic, and refrigerate for at least an hour, or up to 2 days.

4) Preheat oven to 350°. Line 4 cookie sheets with foil or baking parchment. Remove dough from refrigerator one package at a time, and cut in half. If dough is too firm to handle, let soften for a few minutes.

5) Place dough on a lightly floured surface, sprinkle top with a bit of flour, and roll out 1/8-1/4" thick. Dip cookie cutters (or knife) in flour, and cut shapes from dough. Place 1" apart on sheets. Decorate as noted above. (Press scraps of rolled dough together and roll out again. If dough becomes too soft to handle, refrigerate for 15-20 minutes.)

6) Bake 2 sheets at a time for 9-11 minutes, or until dough is set. (After 5 minutes, rotate sheets from rack to rack and back to front to ensure even baking.)

7) Remove sheets from oven and let cool 1-2 minutes. With a thin metal spatula, transfer cookies to wire racks, and let cool completely. Ice as noted above.

8) Stack and store decorated cookies in airtight containers. Store iced cookies in layers separated by sheets of waxed paper.
Yield: about 4 dozen cookies

For Tree Ornaments

Before baking cookies, break some round toothpicks in half. Use a half toothpick for each cookie. With toothpick's broken end, press a small hanger hole in "top" of cookie. Leave toothpick in place during baking to keep dough from filling in the hole. After baking and cooling, gently remove toothpicks. (If necessary, use toothpick to enlarge the hole slightly.) Thread a piece of decorative string or thin ribbon through each hanger hole. Tie ends in a bow.

The Christmas Tree Lamb

by Kathryn Jackson

*O*nce upon a time there was a small white Christmas tree lamb. First he belonged to a grandmother when she was a little girl. Then he belonged to a mother when she was a little girl.

The Christmas tree lamb was brand new when he was given to the grandmother. His fleece was snowy white against the deep green branches of the tree. His black bead eyes seemed to sparkle with excitement. His shining hooves looked as if they were ready to leap from branch to branch. A tiny golden bell on his red satin collar jingled merrily whenever anyone brushed against the tree.

The brand-new lamb's first Christmas was splendid! Everyone said, "That lamb is the prettiest thing on the whole tree!" The grandmother thought so, too, and she stroked his soft fleece every time she walked past him.

The lamb and the grandmother had many splendid Christmases together. But after a while the lamb began to look dusty. And after a while the grandmother was grown up. Then the Christmas lamb was given to the mother.

The mother loved that lamb when she was little. She loved him just as much as the grandmother had. Every year the mother played with him and stroked his soft fleece before she put him on the tree. But one year—*pop!*—a black bead eye came loose and rolled into a corner. The next year—*crack!*—the Christmas lamb lost a leg. Three years later his tiny golden bell fell off. It was swept up, unnoticed, and thrown away with the scraps of wrapping paper and ribbon after all the gifts had been opened.

By the time the mother was grown up and had a little girl of her own, that lamb was in a sorry state! He was gray with dust. He had only one eye, two legs, no collar, and, of course, no bell! But he was still a Christmas lamb, eagerly waiting to go on the tree.

The grandmother picked him up and said, "We can't put him on the tree anymore!"

The mother took him and said, "No, he's nothing to look at now. But how pretty he was, long ago!"

Now, the little girl reached out her hands for the lamb. "How did he look?" she asked.

The grandmother told about his snowy white fleece. The mother told about the golden bell that had jingled so merrily. And the little girl could see for herself that a lamb should have *two* black eyes and *four* legs with shiny hooves.

The little girl carried the lamb into her room. Then she took her treasure box from its hiding place in her closet. Sorting through her treasures, she chose an old toothbrush, a tiny lace handkerchief that had belonged to one of her dolls, and an ice-cream pop stick that she'd saved from last summer.

Using the toothbrush and handkerchief, she brushed and cleaned the lamb's fleece until it was as white as the snow falling outside. After carefully cracking the ice-cream pop stick in half, she glued the pieces to the lamb, and painted a shiny black hoof on the end of each. At the bottom of the box she found a small dark blue bead. It *almost* looks black, she thought, as she put it in place with a tiny drop of glue. And then she threaded a silver jingle bell onto a piece of red ribbon and tied it around the lamb's neck.

When Christmas Eve came, the little girl crept downstairs with the lamb held behind her back. She waited until the grandmother wasn't looking. She waited until the mother wasn't looking. Then she stood on a chair to put the lamb on the Christmas tree. The lamb's new bell jingled merrily.

The grandmother turned and saw the lamb. "Oh!" she gasped. "He looks just as he did when I was a little girl."

The mother looked then, and her eyes glistened. "He looks much finer than he did when I was little!" she said.

The little girl didn't say a word. She was too busy loving the lamb and thinking he was the prettiest thing on the tree. As she stroked his soft white fleece, the lamb's two eyes seemed to sparkle with excitement. His four hooves looked ready to leap from branch to branch. And his new silver bell jingled more merrily than the old gold one ever had. Perhaps that was because the Christmas tree lamb was sure this was going to be the most splendid Christmas of all!

A Christmas Craft
Muffin Cup Stars

*E*asy enough for anyone who can handle a pair of scissors, these pretty stars will shine on gift packages or the branches of the tree. Combine gold and silver muffin baking cups for an especially striking effect.

What you'll need:

* muffin or cupcake baking cups
* 2 or more colors of narrow curling ribbon
* scissors
* glue

—— cut   ⬭ glue

Directions:

1) Slightly flatten 2 muffin cups, place together inside to inside, and cut them to form a 5-pointed star. Cut 3 8-inch pieces of curling ribbon, using at least 2 different colors.

2) Spread glue on inside center of one star. Loop one piece of ribbon and place cut ends on glued area. Place second star, inside down, over first star as shown. Press down.

3) Curl remaining 2 pieces of ribbon with scissors. Cut slit in center of star and pull curled ribbons halfway through. Use the ribbon loop to attach the star to a gift package or to hang it on the tree.

Part Three

SANTA CLAUS

The snow lies white on roof and tree,
Frost fairies creep about,
The world's as still as it can be,
And Santa Claus is out.

He's making haste his gifts to leave,
While the stars show his way,
There'll soon be no more Christmas Eve,
Tomorrow's Christmas Day!

—*anonymous*

Yes, Virginia, There Is a Santa Claus

Several months before Christmas in 1897, a little girl in New York City asked her father a question that he wasn't sure how to answer. So she wrote to the Question and Answer column in their local newspaper, *The New York Sun*, because her father told her that *The Sun* would "give the right answer, as it always does."

Here is the little girl's letter and a portion of the newspaper's response.

Dear Editor,

I am 8 years old.

Some of my friends say there is no Santa Claus. Papa says, "If you see it in *The Sun*, it's so." Please tell me the truth, is there a Santa Claus?

Virginia O'Hanlon

Virginia, your little friends are wrong. They do not believe except what they see. Alas! How dreary would be the world if there were no Santa Claus! It would be as dreary as if there were no Virginias.

Not believe in Santa Claus! You might as well not believe in fairies. You might get your papa to hire men to watch in all the chimneys on Christmas Eve to catch Santa Claus, but even if you did not see Santa Claus coming down, what would that prove? Nobody sees Santa Claus, but that is no sign that there is no Santa Claus. The most real things in the world are those that neither children nor men can see. Did you ever see fairies dancing on the lawn? Of course not, but that's no proof that they are not there. Nobody can conceive or imagine all the wonders there are, unseen and unseeable, in the world.

No Santa Claus! Thank God he lives and lives forever. A thousand years from now, Virginia, nay ten times ten thousand years from now, he will continue to make glad the heart of childhood.

—*The Sun's response, written by Francis P. Church, a reporter and editorial writer who had worked at the paper for 20 years, was an immediate sensation and became one of the most famous editorials ever written. It was reprinted annually by popular demand until 1949 when the paper ceased publishing.*

The First Santa Claus

by Skip Skwarek

Long ago, in a little town in the country that is now called Turkey, lived a kindly young bishop named Nicholas, who wished nothing more than to spend his life doing good deeds. When his parents died, leaving him a small fortune, Nicholas decided to use it to help the needy.

But being quite shy, he always found ways to keep his helpfulness a secret. A family in need of clothing might find a bolt of fine cloth on their doorstep. An elderly woman with no one to care for her would wonder who had left fresh bread and a wedge of good cheese on her hearth. A poor boy without playthings might awaken one morning to discover a pouch of polished stone marbles on his window ledge. For Nicholas, seeing the smiles on the faces of those he helped was reward enough.

One fine spring day, Nicholas heard sobs as he passed the house of a sea captain. Drawing near to a window, he saw the man's daughters in tears. Nicholas knew this should be a happy household as Katherine, the eldest, was to be married in a week's time. Her sisters Maria and Anna had suitors, and were likely to marry before year's end.

"Father's ship has been lost in the storm, and with it our fortunes," he heard Katherine say through her tears.

"But let us rejoice," Maria said, "that he was rescued unharmed."

"Thanks be to God," said Anna, the youngest, as she embraced her sisters. "But you must put off your wedding," she told Katherine, "until Father is safely home."

"There will be no wedding now," Katherine replied, bursting into tears anew.

Nicholas did not stay to hear more, as he knew the reason for Katherine's fresh tears. In those days, it was the custom for the bride's father to give a dowry of money or other valuables to the man who had won his daughter's heart. Since the sea captain's fortunes had been ruined by the loss of his ship, there would be no dowry—and no marriage—for Katherine. Nicholas also knew the captain to be a good and honest man, who had worked tirelessly to raise three fine daughters after the death of his wife.

Late that night when all were asleep, a cloaked figure made its way to the captain's house and tossed something through an open window. The next morning, cries of surprise and delight rang through the house when the sisters discovered a pouch filled with more than enough gold coins for Katherine's dowry. Upon the captain's return, Katherine's marriage was joyfully celebrated.

In a few months' time, Maria's suitor declared his love. On the morning that he was to ask for her hand in marriage, Maria found that a pouch of gold had once again arrived mysteriously. Before long, the astonished captain had two happily married daughters.

Soon after, Anna's suitor asked for her hand. But the captain sadly refused, for surely a pouch of dowry gold would not appear a third time. Heartbroken, Anna threw herself into her chores to ease her misery. By nightfall the house was spotless, and freshly washed stockings hung drying at the hearth.

Unable to sleep, Anna sat at the window long into the night. Had her eyes not been blurred by tears, she might have seen a cloaked figure approach the house and silently climb the tree beside the chimney. At dawn, as she wearily gathered her clean stockings from the hearth, Anna cried out in joy. For out of one stocking tumbled a pouch fat with gold coins.

That very afternoon, everyone in the town came to celebrate as Bishop Nicholas blessed the union of the happy couple. And for Nicholas, as always, the smiling faces were reward enough.

—The tradition of Christmas gift giving can be traced back to Nicholas (A.D. 280–circa 352), bishop of Myra, on the western coast of what is now Turkey. His love of children, and devotion to anonymously helping the needy, inspired various European "Father Christmas" legends during the Middle Ages. Celebrations of Sint Nikolaas *or* Sinter Klaas *were brought to America by Dutch settlers in the early seventeenth century. It is thought that the legend of Nicholas's dowry gifts inspired the modern tradition of hanging stockings by the fire on his feast day (December 6) or Christmas Eve.*

Stocking Song on Christmas Eve

Welcome Christmas, heel and toe,
Here we wait thee in a row.
Come, good Santa Claus, we beg,
Fill us tightly, foot and leg.

Fill us quickly ere you go,
Fill us till we overflow,
That's the way! And leave us more
Heaped in piles upon the floor.

Little feet that ran all day
Twitch in dreams of merry play,
Little feet that jumped at will
Lie all pink and white and still.

See us, how we lightly swing,
Hear us, how we try to sing,
Welcome Christmas, heel and toe,
Come and fill us ere you go!

Here we hang till someone nimbly
Jumps with treasures down the chimney.
Bless us, how he'll tickle us!
Funny old Saint Nicholas.

—*Mary Mapes Dodge*

A Christmas Craft
Paper Bag Santa Puppet

This quick and simple project delivers a bagful of interactive holiday fun! Practice speaking in your Santa voice as you cut and glue.

What you'll need:
* a paper bag that fits over puppeteer's hand
* red construction paper
* white cotton ball and cotton batting or felt
* scissors
* glue
* crayons, markers, or paints

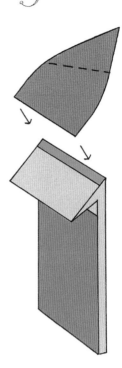

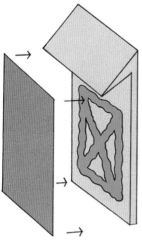

Directions:

1) Cut a piece of red construction paper large enough to cover width and length of bag, beginning just under flap, and glue it to bag.

2) Cut a Santa hat from red construction paper and glue it to top edge of bag's flap. Fold hat's pointed end down at an angle. Glue cotton ball to its tip.

3) Color or paint eyes, nose, and rosy cheeks on flap. Glue strips of batting or felt to flap for eyebrows and mustache. Add batting or felt hatband and whiskers at sides of flap between hat and mustache. Glue batting or felt beard on red paper below flap.

4) Put your hand inside bag, grasp flap, and make Santa's "mouth" move as you "Ho! Ho! Ho!" in your best Santa Claus voice!

------ fold   glue

Santa Claus and the Mouse

One Christmas Eve, when Santa Claus
Came to a certain house
To fill the children's stockings there,
He found a little mouse.

"A Merry Christmas, little friend,"
Said Santa, good and kind.
"The same to you, sir," said the mouse.
"I thought you wouldn't mind

"If I should stay awake tonight
And watch you for a while."
"You're very welcome, little mouse,"
Said Santa with a smile.

And then he filled the stockings up
Before the mouse could wink.
From toe to top, from top to toe,
There wasn't left a chink.

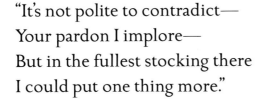

"Now they won't hold another thing,"
Said Santa Claus with pride.
A twinkle shone in mouse's eyes,
But humbly he replied,

"It's not polite to contradict—
Your pardon I implore—
But in the fullest stocking there
I could put one thing more."

"Oh, ho!" laughed Santa. "Silly mouse!
Don't I know how to pack?
By filling stockings all these years,
I should have learned the knack."

And then he took the stocking down
From where it hung so high,
And said, "Now put in one thing more;
I give you leave to try."

The mousie chuckled to himself,
And then he softly stole
Right to the stocking's crowded toe
And gnawed a little hole!

"Now if you please, good Santa Claus,
I've put in one thing more;
For you will own that little hole
Was not in there before."

How Santa Claus did laugh and laugh!
And then he gaily spoke,
"Well, you shall have a Christmas cheese
For that nice little joke."

—*Emile Poulsson*

61

The Bearer of Gifts
by Kenneth Steven

*I*n the very far north of the world is a place called Lapland. And there—where winter days are nearly as dark as night and the snow is at least six feet deep— lived a lonely wood-carver.

All winter the man worked by candlelight, carving useful things. Then he would sell them, traveling across the countryside on a sled pulled by a reindeer.

One night as he was fetching water from the icy stream, the man looked up and saw a brilliant star shining in the eastern sky. "It is bigger than any star I have ever seen," the man said to his dog. "I'm sure it was not there before."

That night the man could not sleep, for the star was shining as brightly as the summer sun. It seemed to be calling to him, inviting him to follow it and find something strange and wonderful.

All night long the man carved by the light of the star, until he had only a scrap of wood left. From it he made a tiny star.

The next morning the man gazed up at the dark gray sky. The star was still there, but now it began to move. Quickly the man filled a sack with his carvings, harnessed the reindeer to his sled, and followed the star across empty lands to the east.

The star led the man through villages where the air was warm and people spoke languages he could not understand. Whenever he was hungry, he was given food in exchange for one of his useful carvings.

And still the star led him on, but it seemed closer and ever more bright. At the top of a steep hill the man stopped. The lights of a town sparkled below. The star hovered overhead, and somehow the man knew that his journey was nearly ended.

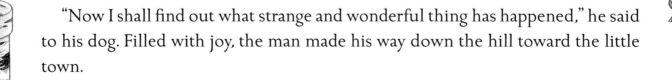

"Now I shall find out what strange and wonderful thing has happened," he said to his dog. Filled with joy, the man made his way down the hill toward the little town.

There was noise everywhere, and spicy scents filled the air. People stared at the odd traveler with his pointy shoes and curious-looking beast. But the man didn't notice. Following the star, he made his way through the town's winding streets. At last he came upon a tiny stable. The star shone directly above it.

Very quietly the man opened the door. He saw two figures beside a manger filled with straw. And upon the straw lay a newborn baby, bathed in a golden light. The man felt so full of peace that he moved closer and knelt beside the baby. A radiance far brighter than the star above the stable shone from the boy child's face.

As the child's parents watched in amazement, a small miracle happened. From head to toe the man glowed with a great warmth, and his rough clothing became thick and soft as it turned from blue to the richest, deepest red.

"You are blessed with a very special child," the man said to the parents. "I must honor him with a gift, for I know in my heart that he shall save the world."

The man went outside and searched his sack for something to give the child. But he had traded all of his fine carvings for food. At the very bottom of the sack the man found the tiny wooden star.

"It is all I have," he whispered to the child, "but I give it in thanks for finding you. I shall never forget this night." And gently kissing the sleeping baby's head, the man went out into the night to begin his long journey home.

The shining star had now disappeared from the sky. But as he traveled through the darkness the man did not feel lonely or afraid, because of the special child he had seen. It was as if the great warmth he had felt were keeping him safe and happy through the long cold journey.

When the man arrived home in Lapland, it was summertime and there were wildflowers blooming and birds singing everywhere. He went from camp to camp, telling the story of the star and his journey and finding the very special baby.

And when the days grew as dark as night and the snow was six feet deep once more, the man began his wood carving again. But now he carved toys for all the children he knew, in memory of the day he had met the child who would save the world.

Then he packed the toys in a sack, harnessed the reindeer, and set off on his sled to deliver a present to every child—to those who had never known the joy of receiving and to those who had never known the joy of giving.

Laplanders say the man is alive to this day, deep in a far north forest, making gifts for all children. Some call him Father Christmas. Others know him as Sinter Klaas or Kriss Kringle. . . .

We call him Santa Claus.

Peppermint Pecan Brownie Bars

Be sure to set out a plate of these for that "jolly old elf" on Christmas Eve.

Three luscious layers—brownie, mint cream, and chocolate glaze—will have good little girls and boys (grown-ups, too!) begging for seconds. Vary the flavor by using spearmint or wintergreen extract, and tint the mint cream green instead of pink. Double the Layer 2 recipe if you wish, and save half for decorative dollops on the baked squares.

Ingredients:

Layer 1:
2 ounces (2 squares) unsweetened chocolate
1/2 cup butter
2 large eggs
1 cup sugar
1/2 cup flour
1/2 cup chopped pecans

Layer 2:
4 tablespoons softened butter
1 1/2 cups confectioners' sugar
2-3 tablespoons cream (or milk)
1 teaspoon peppermint extract
a few drops red food coloring
Layer 3:
3 ounces (3 squares) unsweetened chocolate
3 tablespoons butter

Directions:

1) For Layer 1, preheat oven to 350°. In a small saucepan over low heat, melt chocolate and butter. In a medium bowl, beat eggs and sugar until creamy. Stir in flour and melted chocolate mixture. Combine well. Fold in nuts. Pour batter into a greased and floured 8" square pan and bake for 20 minutes. Remove from the oven and cool completely.

2) For Layer 2, cream butter and sugar in a medium bowl. Mixture will be crumbly. Beat in enough cream to give mixture the consistency of icing. Stir in peppermint and food coloring. Spread over Layer 1 and place pan in freezer.

3) For Layer 3, in a small saucepan over low heat, melt chocolate and butter. Stir well and cool slightly. When Layer 2 is firm, pour Layer 3 over it and tilt pan until Layer 2 is completely covered. Refrigerate until firm. Cut into 2" squares. Store, covered, in refrigerator; serve at room temperature.   Yield: 16 bars

A Visit from Saint Nicholas

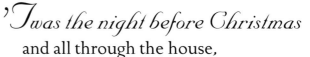

'*Twas the night before Christmas*
    and all through the house,
Not a creature was stirring, not even a mouse.
The stockings were hung by the chimney with care
In hopes that Saint Nicholas soon would be there.
The children were nestled all snug in their beds,
While visions of sugarplums danced in their heads;

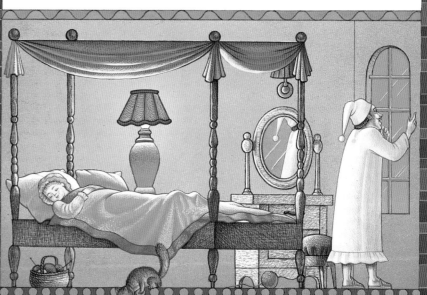

And Mamma in her kerchief and I in my cap,
Had just settled down for a long winter's nap,
When out on the lawn there arose such a clatter,
I sprang from the bed to see what was the matter.
Away to the window I flew like a flash,
Tore open the shutters and threw up the sash.

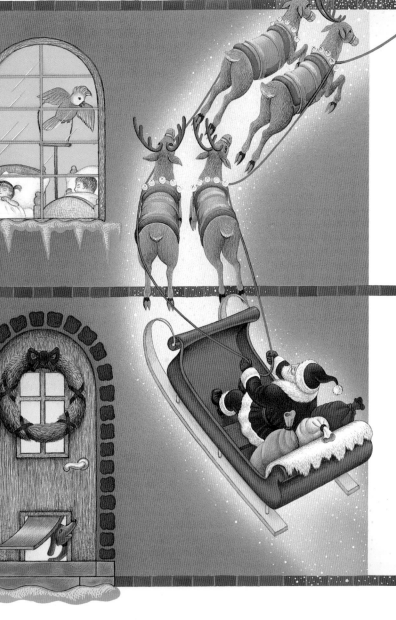

The moon on the breast of the new-fallen snow
Gave the luster of midday to objects below,
When what to my wondering eyes should appear
But a miniature sleigh and eight tiny reindeer,
With a little old driver so lively and quick,
I knew in a moment it must be Saint Nick.

More rapid than eagles his coursers they came,
And he whistled and shouted and called them
    by name:
"Now, Dasher! Now, Dancer! Now, Prancer!
    Now, Vixen!
On, Comet! On, Cupid! On, Donder and Blitzen!
To the top of the porch! To the top of the wall!
Now dash away, dash away, dash away, all!"

As dry leaves that before the wild hurricane fly,
When they meet with an obstacle,
    mount to the sky,
So up to the housetop the coursers they flew,
With the sleigh full of toys and Saint Nicholas, too.
And then, in a twinkling, I heard on the roof
The prancing and pawing of each tiny hoof.

As I drew in my head and was turning around,
Down the chimney Saint Nicholas
    came with a bound.
He was dressed all in fur from his head to his foot,
And his clothes were all tarnished
    with ashes and soot.
A bundle of toys he had flung on his back,
And he looked like a peddler just opening his pack.

His eyes, how they twinkled! His dimples,
    how merry!
His cheeks were like roses, his nose like a cherry!
His droll little mouth was drawn up like a bow,
And the beard on his chin was as white as the snow.
The stump of a pipe he held tight in his teeth,
And the smoke it encircled his head like a wreath.

He had a broad face and a round little belly
That shook, when he laughed,
    like a bowlful of jelly.
He was chubby and plump, a right jolly old elf,
And I laughed when I saw him, in spite of myself.
A wink of his eye and a twist of his head
Soon gave me to know I had nothing to dread.

He spoke not a word but went straight to his work,
And filled all the stockings, then turned with a jerk,
And laying a finger aside of his nose,
And giving a nod, up the chimney he rose.
He sprang to his sleigh, to his team gave a whistle,
And away they all flew like the down of a thistle.

But I heard him exclaim, ere he drove out of sight,
"Happy Christmas to all, and to all a good night!"

—*Clement Clarke Moore*

Part Four

THE NATIVITY

What can I give Him,
Poor as I am?
If I were a shepherd
I would bring a lamb;
If I were a Wise Man
I would do my part;
Yet what can I give Him—
Give my heart.

—*from* In the Bleak Mid-Winter
Christina Rossetti

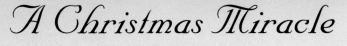

A Christmas Miracle

by Robert D. San Souci

*A*bout the year 1720, when the American Southwest was still under Spanish rule, Padre Antonio Margil was placed in charge of the Mission San Antonio de Valero in the growing town of San Antonio. Most who came here to worship were Spanish settlers, or native Cohuiltecans who had embraced the Christian faith.

As Christmas drew near, worshipers brought gifts of all kinds to the mission. There were buffalo hides and horns, beautifully decorated pottery, wool blankets and rugs, and even handwrought silver jewelry adorned with precious turquoise stones. These were placed near the altar around the brightly painted manger scene, as a special offering to the Christ Child. The little manger itself was empty.

The figure of the Holy Infant would be placed there during the midnight service on Christmas Eve.

On the day before Christmas Eve, Padre Margil noticed an Indian boy, about eight years old, sitting at the back of the church. The youngster was staring glumly at the gifts near the altar. The kindly priest slipped into the pew and sat beside the boy. "What is your name?" he asked.

"Shavano," the boy answered.

"Why do you look so sad, Shavano?" inquired the priest. "Christmas is a time for your heart to be filled with joy."

To the man's dismay, the boy began to cry. "My family is so poor that I have nothing to give the Christ Child."

"The Holy Child doesn't need any gift from you, except your love," said the priest.

But Shavano shook his head stubbornly. "I must give Him something," he insisted.

"Then give Him something that has meaning for you," the priest suggested, "though no one else may see its value."

"What would that be?" asked the boy.

"You must find the answer in your heart," said the priest. "But I know that whatever you choose will be a fine gift." Then he rose, blessed Shavano, and went on his way.

Shavano, remembering that he still had many chores to do at home, also left the church. All afternoon as he swept the earthen floor of the cramped room his family lived in, fetched water, and helped his mother grind corn, he turned over and over in his mind the question of what to bring to the altar.

That evening, when he passed by the mission wall, he saw a small green vine struggling to grow in the parched soil. It looked so tiny against the expanse of sun-burnt adobe. Yet how brave it seemed, too—like hope that takes root in barren ground, like faith that thrives against all odds.

Kneeling, Shavano said, "Here is my gift for the Christ Child." Gently, he dug the vine out of the earth and took it home. He placed it carefully in an old *olla*, a pottery jar that his mother no longer used. Then he carried it to the church.

But when he set the vine in the cracked olla alongside the many rich and brightly colored gifts that surrounded the manger scene, his heart sank. His offering looked little better than a weed. Lowering his head in shame, Shavano reached out to take back his wretched gift.

But his hands had barely touched the olla when Padre Margil called out from behind him, "You must leave it, Shavano. What you have placed by the altar belongs to the Holy Child now."

"But my gift is so poor beside the others," the boy said.

"Anything that is given with love is beyond price," said the priest. "Now go home; it is growing dark. Tomorrow, bring your parents to the Christmas pageant. After that, we will say special prayers as we place the Christ Child in the manger and offer our gifts to Him."

On Christmas Eve, Shavano and his parents joined the crowd in the plaza in front of the mission to watch some of their friends and neighbors act out a *pastorela*. The Nativity play told how shepherds set out to see the Christ Child on the first Christmas and how the devil tried to stop them. At last, the angel Gabriel struck down the devil and brought things to a happy end.

As the audience began cheering the pastorela players, Shavano shuddered. The moment he had been dreading was at hand. Now it was time to go into the church and offer the gifts. Surely everyone would laugh at his miserable vine.

The boy lagged behind as he followed Padre Margil into the church. The priest carried the figure of the Holy Child, ready to place it in the waiting manger.

Suddenly Padre Margil cried out, "*Milagro!* A miracle!" and dropped to his knees before the altar. Behind him, the crowd fell to their knees. Only Shavano remained standing, staring at the altar.

Overnight, his vine had grown a thousandfold! It wrapped around the manger and covered the gifts near the altar. Its leaves were lush and green, and among them glistened countless brilliant red berries.

With trembling hand, Padre Margil beckoned to Shavano. The priest placed the painted figure of the Christ Child in the boy's hands. "Put the Infant on the altar," whispered the priest. Tenderly, Shavano set the figure in the manger. It seemed to him, just for a moment, the Infant's red lips—the color of the berries that grew all around—curled into a smile. Shavano smiled, too.

"You see, Shavano," said the priest, "your faith and love have worked a very special miracle."

Behind the boy and the priest, the worshipers who had crowded into the church bowed their heads in prayer and joy. Each felt that he or she had been touched by heaven in a special way on this most blessed of Christmases.

—*In parts of Texas, coral honeysuckle, sometimes called the Margil vine, remains an important symbol of Christmas. There are those who say that, until the miracle at the mission, the vine had never been known to bear fruit. But since then, it has borne clusters of radiant red berries every Christmas. People continued to worship at Mission San Antonio de Valero until 1793. After 1801, the mission compound was used as a military outpost and renamed the Alamo. It still stands today.*

A Christmas Carol

Away In a Manger

The carol's words were originally attributed to Martin Luther, but may be the work of an anonymous poet, first published in 1885 in *A Little Children's Book*—over three hundred years after Luther's death.

Music James R. Murray

Gently

1. A - way in a man - ger, no crib for a bed, The
2. The cat - tle are low - ing, the poor Ba - by wakes, But
3. Be near me, Lord Je - sus, I ask Thee to stay, Close

lit - tle Lord Je - sus laid down His sweet head; The
lit - tle Lord Je - sus no cry - ing He makes, I
by me for - ev - er, and love me, I pray; Bless

stars in the sky — Looked down where He lay, The
love Thee, Lord Je - sus! Look down from the sky, And
all the dear chil - dren in Thy ten - der care, And

lit - tle Lord Je - sus, A - sleep on the hay.
stay by my cra - dle, Till morn - ing is nigh.
take us to heav - en To live with Thee there.

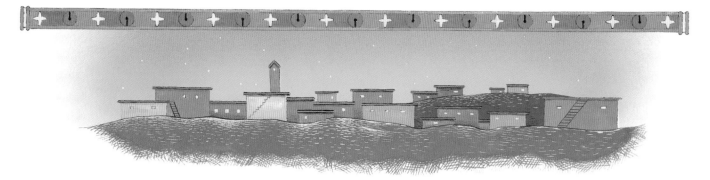

There were in the same country shepherds staying in the fields, keeping watch over their flocks by night. And, lo, the angel of the Lord came upon them, and the glory of the Lord shone round about them, and they were much afraid.

"Fear not," the angel said to them. "For I bring you good tidings of a great joy that is coming to all people. For to you is born this day in the city of David, a Savior, who is Christ the Lord. And this shall be a sign to you: You shall find the babe wrapped in swaddling clothes, lying in a manger."

And suddenly there was with the angel a multitude of the heavenly host, praising God and saying, "Glory to God in the highest, and on earth, good will toward men."

The Visit of the Wise Men

Now, when Jesus was born in Bethlehem of Judea, in the days of Herod the king, there came Wise Men from the east to Jerusalem, asking: "Where is He that is born King of the Jews? For we have seen His star in the east and are come to worship Him."

When Herod the king heard these things, he was troubled, and all Jerusalem with him. And when he had gathered all the chief priests and scribes of the people together, he asked them where Christ should be born. "In Bethlehem of Judea," they said. "For thus it is written by the prophet:

And you, Bethlehem, in the land of Judah, are not the least among the princes of Judah. For out of you shall come a Governor that shall rule my people Israel."

Then Herod sent secretly for the Wise Men and asked them what time the star had appeared. And he sent them to Bethlehem, saying, "Go and search carefully for the young child, and when you have found him, bring me word, that I may come and worship him also."

When they had heard the king, they departed. And, lo, the star which they saw in the east went before them till it came and stood over the place where the young child was. When they saw the star, they rejoiced with great joy. And when they came into the house, they saw the young child with Mary, His mother, and they fell down and worshiped Him and presented gifts to Him: gold, frankincense, and myrrh. And being warned by God in a dream that they should not return to Herod, they departed and returned to their own country by another way.

—*Matthew 2*

The Birth of Jesus

And it came to pass in those days that a decree went out from Caesar Augustus, the emperor in Rome, that all the world should be taxed.

So everyone went to be taxed, each to his own city. And Joseph went up from Galilee, out of the city of Nazareth, into Judea, to the city of David, which is called Bethlehem, because he was of the house and family of David, to be taxed with Mary, his wife, who was soon to have a child.

And it came to pass that while they were there, the day arrived for her child to be born. She brought forth her firstborn son and wrapped him in swaddling clothes and laid him in a manger, because there was no room for them in the inn.

The Friendly Beasts

Jesus, our brother, strong and good,
Was humbly born in a stable rude.
The friendly beasts around Him stood,
Jesus, our brother, strong and good.

"I," said the donkey, all shaggy and brown,
"I carried His mother uphill and down,
I carried her safely to Bethlehem town.
I," said the donkey, all shaggy and brown.

"I," said the cow, all white and red,
"I gave Him my manger for His bed,
I gave Him my hay to pillow His head.
I," said the cow, all white and red.

"I," said the sheep with the curly horn,
"I gave Him my wool for a blanket warm,
He wore my coat on Christmas morn.
I," said the sheep with the curly horn.

When the angels had gone away from them into heaven, the shepherds said to one another, "Let us go into Bethlehem and see this thing that has come to pass, which the Lord has made known to us."

They went with haste and found Mary and Joseph, and the babe lying in a manger. And when they had seen it, they made known throughout the land what they had been told concerning this child. And all who heard it marveled at the things which were told to them by the shepherds. But Mary kept all these things and pondered them in her heart.

—Luke 2

"I," said the camel, all yellow and black,
"Over the desert upon my back,
  I brought Him a gift in the Wise Man's pack.
  I," said the camel, all yellow and black.

"I," said the dove from the rafters high,
"I cooed Him to sleep so He would not cry.
  We cooed Him to sleep, my mate and I.
  I," said the dove from the rafters high.

So every beast, by some good spell,
In the stable dark was glad to tell
Of the gift he gave Immanuel—
The gift he gave Immanuel.

—*attributed to Robert Davis*

Benjamin, Boy of Bethlehem
by Dianne T. Shepherd

Benjamin ran with all his might. His bare feet scarcely touched the hard-packed dirt of the alley that he'd ducked into, to escape the Roman guards. Glancing quickly over his shoulder, he was relieved to see he'd lost them. He hid himself in a doorway and eagerly bit into the apple he'd stolen from the peddler's cart. Except for the small bowl of bread and milk he and his grandfather had shared early that morning, he hadn't eaten anything all day. The apple was sweet and juicy, and Benjamin wished he'd had time to steal more than just one.

Finishing it, he walked to the end of the alley, which opened onto one of the town's main roads. Carts, camel caravans, and throngs of people on foot crowded the road. It looked as if the whole world were coming to Bethlehem tonight. Stepping out of the shadows of the alley, Benjamin squinted as he looked up into the clear night sky. The moon and stars shone brilliantly, and directly above him was the brightest star he'd ever seen. He gazed at it in wonder for a moment and then slipped into the noisy crowd, hoping to steal something else to eat.

Benjamin had begun exploring the streets of Bethlehem almost as soon as he'd learned to walk. His parents died of the plague when he was a baby, and he'd lived with his grandfather ever since. They'd always had more than enough to eat when his grandfather had been able to work as a scribe, reading and writing letters for people who hadn't been taught how to do it themselves. Every day of the week, except the Sabbath, his grandfather had taken his writing tools and Benjamin to the bazaar, where he did business until the last peddlers packed up their carts at twilight. But his eyes had weakened, and he could no longer see well enough to read or write. Now Benjamin went alone to the bazaar every day. Small—but fast and strong—for a boy of eight, he sometimes found work loading carts. But the few coins he earned bought very little food, and so he stole. Luckily, he knew every hidden courtyard and alleyway in Bethlehem, or the Roman guards would have easily captured him.

The streets were less crowded now, as the hour was late. Benjamin saw that he'd wandered into the outskirts of Bethlehem, the part of the town he liked best. Here there weren't many buildings, just a few inns, and stables for the farm animals. And beyond were grass-covered rolling hills where shepherds tended flocks of sheep. Benjamin loved to lie in the tall grass and stare up at the stars.

But just then he was startled by the sound of a baby's cry. He looked around and saw a stable nearby with bright golden light shining from its open door. He stole closer and peered inside. Amidst piles of straw sat a plainly dressed young woman, cradling a newborn baby in her arms. Three men, wearing fine robes encrusted with jewels, presented gifts as they knelt before the baby and bowed their heads. *What child could this be*, Benjamin wondered, *born in a stable but worshiped by men dressed like kings?* Astonished, he drew back and saw a group of shepherds approaching the stable.

One of them stepped toward Benjamin. "Is this the birthplace of the Son of God?" the shepherd asked. Before Benjamin could find the words to answer, the shepherds saw the baby and hurried into the stable.

"The Son of God?" Benjamin repeated aloud. "Why would the Son of God be born in a stable?" Puzzled, he walked back to the road. "Grandfather will know what is happening," he told himself and started for home.

When he turned onto the road where the bazaar was held during the day, he saw two Roman guards talking and laughing loudly. He recognized them just as they looked up and noticed him.

"Halt, boy! What are you doing out so late?" called one of them.

"He's the little thief we were chasing before," shouted the other. "After him!"

Benjamin turned and started to run, but one of the guards grabbed him by the shoulder and held him firmly. "Well, you slippery little fish," sneered the man, "you're caught now, and you'll pay dearly for that stolen apple."

Trapped in the guard's viselike grip, Benjamin was dragged along as the men walked down the road. "And how does King Herod expect us to find the right newborn baby in all of Bethlehem?" one of the guards grumbled. "Besides, what terrible harm could a tiny baby do to us, the unconquerable Romans?"

"I know not, Flavius," responded the other, "but we'd better find this so-called Son of God or we'll be eating our next meal in the dungeon."

At the words "Son of God," Benjamin's ears pricked up. That was what the shepherds had called the baby! What the guards had said convinced Benjamin that the baby was in danger. He decided at once what he must do. The guards were joking with each other again, and the hand gripping Benjamin relaxed just a little; but it was enough for Benjamin to pull free.

He raced down the road with the guards right behind, furious that this small boy had escaped from them twice. Benjamin ran faster than he'd ever run before.

He dodged behind buildings and through dark courtyards. Rounding a corner, he realized, too late, that he'd returned to the road that circled the outskirts of the city. There were no more buildings to hide behind. He heard the guards' voices getting closer and knew he'd be caught again if he didn't find a hiding place immediately. Scanning the open field across the road, Benjamin spotted a small haystack and sprinted to it. He burrowed into the hay just as the guards raced around the corner and out into the road. They trotted to the edge of the field and stopped within a few feet of the haystack.

"That little tramp! Where could he have gone?" muttered one of the guards.
"Let him go, Colius," replied the other. "We'd better find that baby."
They turned and headed back toward the center of the town.

Benjamin waited until the clanging sound of the guards' armor faded away, then sat up and spit hay out of his mouth. *I've got to warn the baby*, he thought. With hay still clinging to his clothes, Benjamin raced toward the maze of alleys that he knew so well. He had no idea which way the guards had gone and certainly didn't want to run into them, so he kept to the shadows cast by buildings and ran as quietly as he could.

He came to his own neighborhood before long, and as he neared his home he saw the soft glow of an oil lamp lighting the doorway. The lamp was a familiar signal. It meant that his grandfather was still awake and worrying that he was out at such a late hour. Benjamin slowed to a guilty walk. He had been taught to respect his elders and knew that causing his grandfather to worry was wrong.

And so he headed for the doorway, planning to tell his grandfather about the helpless baby. Stepping inside, he saw that his grandfather was fast asleep. With a quiet sigh of relief, Benjamin blew out the lamp and trotted back out to the road. "Don't let them find the baby," he whispered over and over to himself as he picked up his pace.

At the road that led to the stable, Benjamin skidded to an abrupt halt and ducked into a doorway. His worst fears had come true! The guards were at the door of the inn next to the stable. His heart hammered as he watched them question the innkeeper, who first shook his head and then pointed to the stable. All at once, Benjamin felt a tremendous fear for the baby. And just as suddenly, he knew what to do.

The guards walked back into the road and were approaching the stable when Benjamin darted from the doorway. "Hail, creeping Roman snails!" he shouted. "You call yourselves guards and yet cannot catch a small boy such as I!"

"It's the apple thief again," growled Colius. "Let me get my hands on him."

"Ignore him," snapped Flavius. "We have more important business than to chase after little beggars like him."

"A thief I may be, but I beg only God's help," Benjamin whispered as he bent down, picked up a handful of pebbles, and hurled them at the guards. They struck their mark, and the guards cried out in surprise. Muttering angrily, they turned and started toward Benjamin.

Backing slowly away from them, Benjamin continued his taunts. "So you think you might be able to catch up with me this time, do you? A snail cannot move as fast as a rabbit, and you cannot move as fast as a snail, so how will you catch me?"

Benjamin shouted more insults to make the guards even angrier. He didn't want them to think they could scare him off just by chasing him for a short distance. He wanted to lead them far away from the stable.

"You are like muzzled dogs. You try hard to frighten with your loud growls because you cannot bite."

"I'll show you who can bite," sputtered Flavius as he broke into a run.

"Old women!" shouted Benjamin as he turned and began clambering up a steep, rocky hillside, with the guards close behind. He was panting for breath by the time he reached the flat top of the hill. Ahead he saw a thick grove of trees where, with a little luck, he might lose them. He glanced back at the guards struggling up the hill under the weight of their heavy armor, grinned, and sprinted for the trees.

Benjamin disappeared into the grove just as the guards reached the hilltop. He quickly scooped up several small stones and then climbed to the top of a tree near the edge of the grove. Hidden by its leafy boughs, Benjamin peered out and saw the guards pointing at the grove. Their faces were red and dripping with perspiration. Their angry voices grew louder as they approached the trees.

They moved toward the tree where Benjamin hid. When they were just a few steps away, he took one of the stones and threw it farther into the grove.

"Did you hear that?" whispered Colius.

Benjamin threw another stone in the same direction. The guards pointed as they heard the sounds. Benjamin threw another stone and another.

"He's going that way!" exclaimed Flavius, and they crashed off into the grove.

When they were out of sight, Benjamin silently dropped from the tree and ran down the hill to the stable. Stepping inside, he looked around and his heart sank. Except for a donkey, a cow, and a few chickens, it was empty. *Could this be the same stable?* he wondered. "It has to be the same one!" he cried out. "But where is the Son of God?"

From one of the dark stalls stepped a man, followed by the woman with the child. "You are the boy who led the guards away from us," the man said softly.

Speechless, Benjamin could only nod his head.

"Your voice alerted us that the guards were here," the man continued. "We had been told of Herod's plan to kill the baby and were preparing to leave, but we hid when we heard you taunting the guards. You risked your life for the Son of God, child, and you shall be repaid many times over."

"But you must go now," Benjamin finally managed to say. "They may come back at any moment."

"Yes, and thank you." Quickly, the man led the woman and the baby away.

Benjamin turned and walked out of the stable into the dawn of the new day.

A Christmas Carol
I Heard the Bells on Christmas Day

Written in 1864, Longfellow's rousing poem was later set to this very appropriate music; the bass sounds like a bell ringing.

Words Henry Wadsworth Longfellow / Music J. Baptiste Calkin

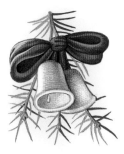

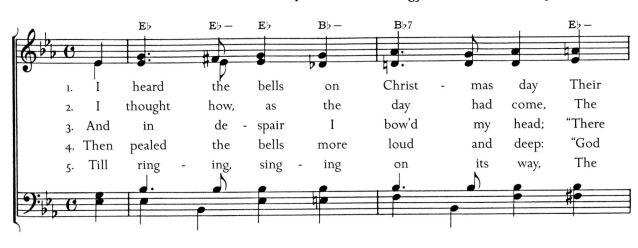

1. I heard the bells on Christ - mas day Their
2. I thought how, as the day had come, The
3. And in de - spair I bow'd my head; "There
4. Then pealed the bells more loud and deep: "God
5. Till ring - ing, sing - ing on its way, The

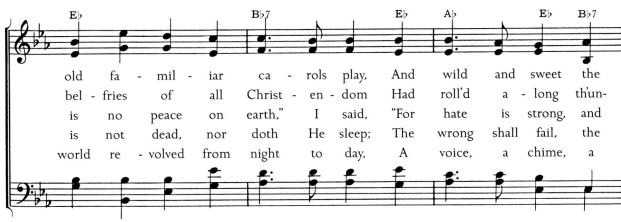

old fa - mil - iar ca - rols play, And wild and sweet the
bel - fries of all Christ - en - dom Had roll'd a - long th'un -
is no peace on earth," I said, "For hate is strong, and
is not dead, nor doth He sleep; The wrong shall fail, the
world re - volved from night to day, A voice, a chime, a

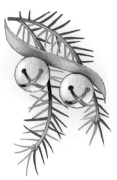

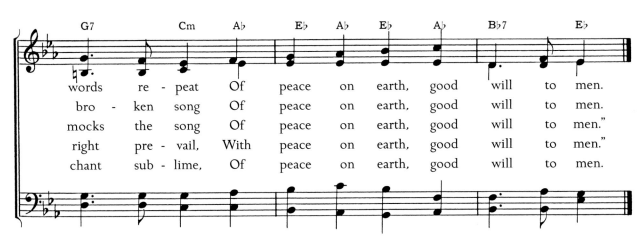

words re - peat Of peace on earth, good will to men.
bro - ken song Of peace on earth, good will to men.
mocks the song Of peace on earth, good will to men."
right pre - vail, With peace on earth, good will to men."
chant sub - lime, Of peace on earth, good will to men.

101